TOO MANY TOYS!

Heidi Deedman

For Eugene,
who has just the right number of toys.

First published 2015 by Walker Books Ltd
87 Vauxhall Walk, London SE11 5HJ

10 9 8 7 6 5 4 3 2 1

© 2015 Heidi Deedman

The right of Heidi Deedman to be identified as author/illustrator of this work has
been asserted by her in accordance with the Copyright, Designs and Patents Act 1988

This book has been typeset in Alghera and handlettered by the author.

Printed in Malaysia

British Library Cataloguing in Publication Data:
a catalogue record for this book is available from the British Library

ISBN 978-1-4063-4681-7

www.walker.co.uk

TOO MANY TOYS!

Heidi Deedman

🐻 WALKER BOOKS
AND SUBSIDIARIES
LONDON · BOSTON · SYDNEY · AUCKLAND

When Lulu was a baby
she was given a very special
one-and-only toy –

a lovely, fluffy teddy bear.

Lulu named him Jupiter

and she loved him
very, very much.

As Lulu grew, she was given more toys to play with.

And more toys

and MORE toys.

But no matter how many toys she got, Jupiter was always her favourite.

When Lulu was five years old she had a birthday party. There was cake, balloons and lots of games.

There were also LOTS of presents, which meant ...

LOTS MORE TOYS!

It was getting harder and harder to find room for all of Lulu's toys.

The shelves were full.

The toy box wouldn't close.

Breakfast time was messy.

TV time
was noisy!

Playtime
was rowdy.

Bathtime
was splashy.

And then . . .

IT WAS CHRISTMAS!

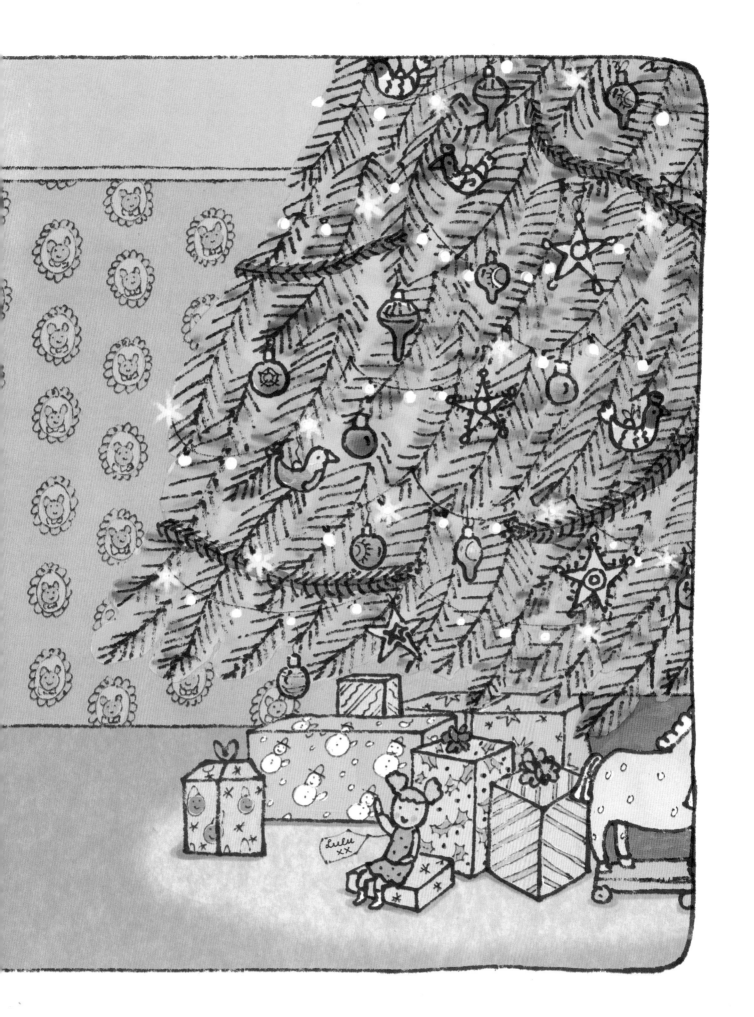

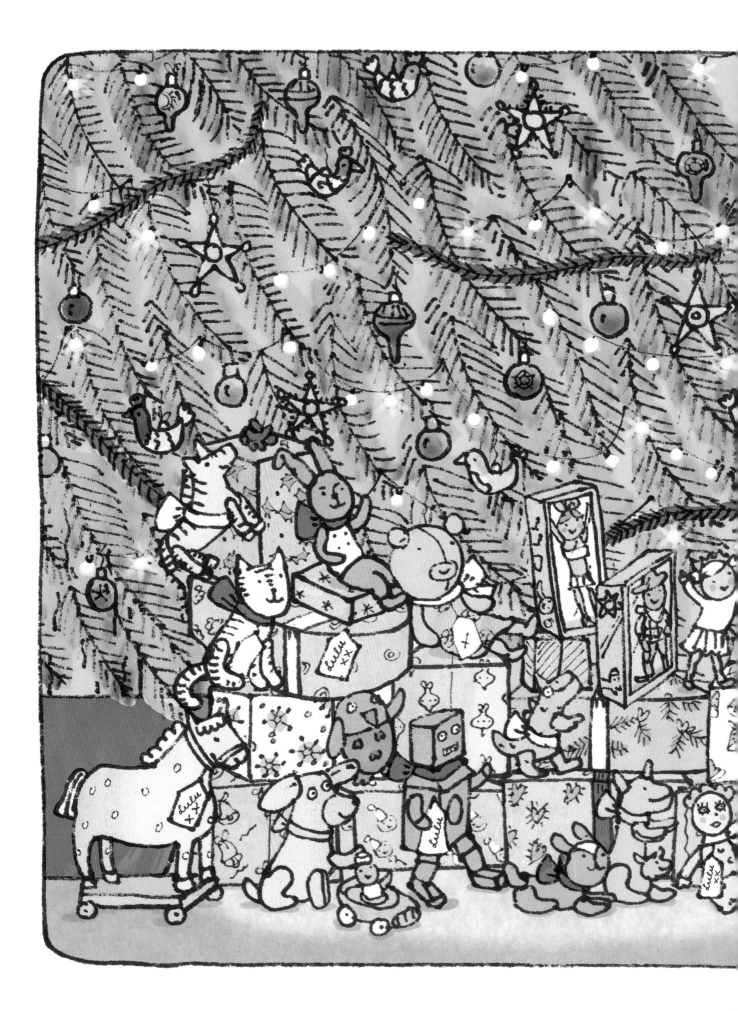

Lulu just had too many toys!

"What are we going to do, Jupiter?" said Lulu. "I can't play with everybody!"

She thought hard.

She made up her mind.

Lulu had a plan...

She put all her toys together in a GREAT BIG ENORMOUS pile.
(Have you ever seen so many toys?)

Now she was ready for...

All her friends came
from far and wide.

And Lulu gave away . . .

a big, soft dog,

the truck (with a dog, a pig and a teddy girl),

a walking, talking robot,

a doll that said "Mama",

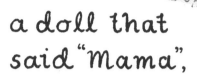

two more dolls,

even more dolls,

three soldiers (and their horse),

a musical monkey,

a family of dogs,

a lion with
a curly
mane,

her doll's house
and all the furniture,

a sort of gonk,

the stripy cat,

a box of cars,

the big kite,

and lots more
until all the
toys were gone.

Did Lulu keep
anything at all?

Of course she did.

She kept Jupiter,
 her one-and-only.
He was much too special
 to give away!

"Jupiter – you are all I need,"
said Lulu.

Still...
There might be a tiny bit of space...
for just a few more toys...
next Christmas.